TR.8C

Cover artwork and design by Jamie Ibson

Published by Petrichor Press, an imprint of Amity Studios, LLC

Manitou Springs, Colorado, USA

eBook ISBN: 978-1-949906-18-9
Trade paperback ISBN: 978-1-949906-27-1

TR.8C

"TR ground units, four minutes and counting. Sparrow disembarks from target grid Gama on Track Qav-4 for removal of assets. Check to acknowledge."

"I'm a little, ugh, busy," I grunted under my breath, and snaked my arm around the SimNAC's throat. I tightened up before it could slip its slimy hide from my grasp and twisted my torso around until it was completely off balance. I dropped my bodyweight, folding the pale-skinned thing in half over my knee with an audible crack. I finished it off with a twist of its neck and dropped the limp body to the alien forest floor.

I touched the embedded chip inside my cheek to open my comm. "Check," I responded, then touched to end transmission.

On Qav-4, SimNACs grew a lot smaller than the humanoids I remembered, but that wasn't any different than the last termination expedition to Qav-3. Their name had evolved from the first sighting on Qav-1, where they'd been referred to as "aliens," which never set well with me. They aren't alien to their world. We are. When similar beings were found on Qav-2, "alien" was dropped in favor of "SimNAC."

They were similar, native, alien, and common among all Qav stars. The bipedal terrestrials seemed to get shorter each time. These new beings on

Qav-4 were wiry, quick, and their slick skin made it hard to get hold of them in a fight. And the smell! Their skin looked like reused, curdled amniotic fluid from the pods inside Mother on New Hope.

Beyond the alien's dead body, I looked only at the bubbling font of pure, natural water it had been guarding. The water tripped and gurgled over stones and formed a glorious crystal pool. I used the camera on my visor to click an image and sent it to the Sparrow. I dropped to my knees and took a flask from my belt to fill with water, being careful not to touch the mouth of the container to any of the pebbles, moss, or algae close by. The sample had to be pure, as clean as it appeared to me now.

Such resources had gone dry decades after the global war on Earth, as if one apocalyptic event wasn't enough to send what was left of the planet's survivors onto a mega station like New Hope.

Only a few minutes remained for me to get back to meet the Sparrow. The beautiful, fresh, rare water beckoned to be tasted. Surely I had a few seconds to spare to test the flavor myself? I tried to fit my hand into the little pool, my dark skin contrasted with the pebbles, making them seem brighter. I didn't want to take off any of my gear, so I balanced carefully, leaned close to the font, and pulled in a long, crisp drink through my lips. The spring didn't disappoint. I might have found the best source of water humankind had accessed in centuries.

I filled my mouth again, intending to hold the bounty there while I ran for transport, but it was too cold against my palate. I swallowed and slammed my eyes shut, rubbing my tongue over the roof of my mouth to warm it up. A tear rolled down my cheek, and I squinted for a moment until the pain subsided. The SimNAC had expired in the moments I stole at the pool side. Its dark eyes had dulled in the pasty skin of the face, and its legs had curled up to its belly, making it appear deflated. They all looked tiny without their arms spread and the membranous webbing spanning beneath. I nudged it with the toe of my boot to make sure it wasn't playing dead. There was no movement. I secured the flask to my belt and broke into a run, hopping over bushes, small trees, and boulders. More TR units merged in my path, and we sprinted as one, leveling a trail of flattened flora toward the lowered bay door of the Sparrow. We racked our weapons, took the designated jump seats from the earlier drop, and buckled in, the clicks and snaps rattling atop sounds from the ship's engines. The bay door hissed into motion, sealing us off from the golden ambient star lighting Qav-4. I had the habit of looking at the other seats and trying to remember which fellow TR unit sat there. More importantly, to me anyway, was that each was filled as it was before the drop, and that one seat in particular was occupied. That wasn't the case today.

Unit TR.8B hadn't returned. My heart dropped. Of 18 units, she was the one who hadn't come back. I covered my heartbreak, fidgeting with the buckle of my harness. TR units are restricted from attempting to bond with another. The engineering had failed for years, as the Parents attempted to rid TRs of social needs and desires. Although there were numerous remaining Non-Aug males among the Parents' ranks, they'd thrown in the towel and stopped engineering TR males decades ago because they'd proved more problematic than females. I don't know the details. These days, we shouldn't feel any longings at all, if our individual engineering is a success. Our makeup dictates we aren't prone to "outdated human urges" like skin hunger, camaraderie, or even friendship. The urge to mate was stripped out of us first, since the Parents considered that the most problematic of traits to pass on.

TRs do not need to breed.I didn't know which abandoned bit of humanity was worse to go without.

TR.8B and I had joked about our mutual defectiveness, hiding in order to share time together. As personalities went, I was the calm one, and she was the hothead. We weren't the only TRs to break the rules. Friendship was the kicker for me. Embraces—simple hugs—took care of skin hunger for the most part. Friendship, though? Friendship I couldn't live without. The sneaking around and spending time together to fill needs would have rendered us flawed and inoperative, had we ever been caught. B and I had seen other TRs sneak off together. Being caught doing these little things was all it would take for the Parents to declare us abominations.

If I ever wanted a friend, I was a failed product.

Abominable me.

"Today was a great day for you TRs. Your confirmation of clean water on Qav-4 means salvation for what remains of the human race. Excellent job." Mercury Johnston, a non-augmented human who stood nearly three feet shorter than me and weighed about as much as one of my legs, beamed at us, turning to look at each TR and smile as the Sparrow lit its internal systems in preparation to ascend through the thick atmosphere of Qav-4.

To leave my friend behind.

As I expected, Johnston didn't react when her eyes glanced past the dark, empty space where TR.8B should have been. My gaze was repeatedly drawn there, despite how hard I fought to hold composure. B was still outside on the ground. No matter her injuries, or lack thereof, it wasn't bred into TRs to quit our duty or mission.

The fact that our parent race gave up on us so easily, and made such a simple time of it by replacing us like worn or broken tools, made my blood alternate between icing over and boiling. I toyed with the control pads inside my cheek to fight the urge to ask about TR.8B. We all knew what happened when defects showed up. We'd all witnessed them decommission a TR unit. We would be gassed and incinerated. That was one of the Parents' tactics to keep us focused. That didn't make my day any easier, or my heart hurt any less.

Johnston went on with her praise of us, her words blending into a meaningless din as I fidgeted, worried, and stared at her. Her pock-marked skin was near-black, unlike smooth TR skin, a rusted brown hue like the coffee the Parents drank. Like other NonAugs I'd seen, she had thick, black hair growing from her scalp. Where we TRs never grow hair, Johnston's was a wonder of draping spirals. I sometimes caught myself watching it as she moved, her tresses swaying and clinging to her uniform in places.

We had eye color in common. Every human I'd seen had the same eyes as mine, a brown so deep it appeared black sometimes. The goal is for TRs to be created identical. The Parents thought they'd succeeded there, but we TRs could tell each other apart easily. Muscle mass, height, skin tone; we are indistinguishable to the Parents.To them we're a uniform force created and deployed to fight for the future colonies of humankind—TRs, NonAugs, and all of those in between. TRs are not to be labeled as Human. We are units. We are TR, descendants of A, then B, and so on. Knowing our history is our responsibility, the same as knowing the history of Man. We read a lot from salvaged cultural archives. We watch a lot of programs. The survival system implemented when Humans evacuated Earth was breaking down, never meant to last as long as the New Hope had in the first place.

The Parents were good and tired of drinking recycled urine, although I couldn't have told you the difference before today at the spring.

"At least two hours with Mother tonight. Clear?"

"Clear," I copied with my fellow units. We didn't need much rest normally, but the drop to clear the track to harvest water samples on Qav-4 had been more rigorous than others. More SimNACs to fight off.

Johnston continued, "You've done great things on Qav-4. With the data gathered, the last of our race has a chance. Just as the other Qav planet colonies, this remaining quarter of us on the New Hope will have a new home. Lives will be saved if we keep working fast," she said, with relief evident in her voice. "Although you TR units are immune from the deadly epidemic attacking what's left of our race, your Parents' numbers dwindle and decrease by the day." She paused, looking at each of us.

When her watery eyes crossed mine, I looked away, remembering that I couldn't betray the turmoil I felt because of B's absence.

The fact that Mercury Johnston and the other Parents were under bio attack, dying from a rogue, unknown sickness, was horrifying. They needed clean air and water to survive, but the systems on the ship were contaminated. Many of them had died. That kind of loss was something TRs dealt with every time one of us was left behind. I wasn't as versed in stoicism as the others, apparently.

I glanced across at TR.8I and 8S. They watched me and knew full well what I was going through. If either of them didn't make it back, they'd be wounded. They were grateful it wasn't them. I searched TR faces, recognizing more pairs. More hidden friendships.

Johnston continued, "Stay strong. Fight well. But you need your rest for our upcoming return."

I didn't feel the drain, but my power level was designed to last weeks, even months, when I could conserve energy. Sleep worked, too. Mother worked faster.

I couldn't imagine a stint of regenerating incubation inside Mother, back on New Hope, while I stared through the transparent partition from my chamber into the emptiness of TR.8B's. If Johnston had her way, all of us TR units would plug into Mother, and a new unit would join us before the next drop. She would replace B without a second thought. It was infuriating. For the first time in my short life, I felt turmoil. Panic. Fear of loss. The tug of liftoff was like ice down my spine.

I made a decision to act, and it felt like someone else controlled my movements. I released the belts securing me to my seat, dropped my visor down again, and rose slowly to my feet. Johnston stopped speaking and looked up at me with huge, startled eyes. The Parent's eyes grew vastly wider as she craned her neck to look up at me.

"Sit and secure, TR.8C. Now."

"I can't!" My voice was filled with all the emotions that had torn at me since returning to the Sparrow.

Johnston clapped her hands over her tender ears as I sprinted past, still yelling. "I can't leave her!" I snatched my weapon from the rack on the way by, dropping the strap across my chest. I slammed my palm against the pad to lower the bay door, which stalled the ship's lift. The seal squealed, and air hissed past my face, as light flashed inside the hold once more. Alarms blared. My heart pounded in my chest like it was trying to beat its way out. Nothing happened fast enough. I shoved my hands into the growing opening and pushed with all my might. The urge to sprint and search through the alien terrain on Qav-4 twitched through my blood. I slammed my shoulder against the door, forcing the opening wide enough to climb through. My armored vest hung up briefly, but I wiggled my way through. First my head and chest, then one leg. When I yanked my other leg through, I found myself dangling by one hand about ten meters above the surface. All my weight on the top of the bay door was too much for the hydraulics, and the hinge mechanism released, the door ramping completely open, with me struggling to maintain a grip with one hand.

I reached to bring my weapon around front and off safety, staring down at about a dozen SimNACs who'd come running toward the sound of the Sparrow's liftoff. They snarled and howled, lifting both arms and leaping as if to grab onto my swinging boots. I fired into the herd, cutting down a few in the center. I nearly lost my hand hold on the door when something smashed my fingers. I choked up my grip as I fought to hold on.

Johnston's face came into view briefly over the ramp of the door as she peered over the edge at me, clinging to the base of the bay door. I'd never seen her look so determined before. She gritted her teeth and kicked down with the heel of her boot, smashing my fingers again.

I considered letting go of my rifle, grabbling onto her foot, and dragging her closer. I could yank her down the ramp of the door. Drop her into the churning, growling mass of SimNACs below.

I didn't.

I let go of the door. Training had prepared me for falls much longer than this one. A fall into a clutch of riled up terrestrials was a new element, however. I saw no need to wait, squeezing the trigger and sending a fast burst of lead toward the enemy before my boots hit the ground. I dropped like a boulder toward the lush overgrowth and hostiles of Qav-4, trembling inside with bottled-up adrenaline. Before landing, I bent the joints in my legs, then touched down with my feet barely contacting the alien brush, transferring the force of the drop as I rolled until the inertia faded. I came to my feet with my weapon shouldered, found my first target, and dropped it with a headshot.

I'd landed about 15 meters from the closest terrestrial. They kept coming, and I took them out one at a time with careful shots, advancing on them until none were standing.

Quick and quiet, I ran through the fallen SimNACs, kicking them over onto their backs so I could see their necks, checking their throats carefully for arterial flow. One had a belly wound and still drew breath. I finished the sanitization of the site to ensure my safety, backing away from the bodies. Nothing moved in the brush, but I couldn't be sure that at least one SimNAC hadn't run off.

Being alone without my team meant a lot more uncertainty. That said, this wasn't a fresh drop. My entire team had just come through here, returning to the dropship, so the terrain was the same, and my assessment went quickly. Training dictates we ensure our surroundings are safe at all times, but in this case, I'd proceed as if I was being hunted. That meant using silence rather than fire power when possible.

Calm and in control, I secured my weapon at my back.

The Sparrow stayed the departure course, the sound of the engines growing faint. I wasn't surprised that the ship didn't stop or land again. It was just as easy for the Parents to replace two TR units as it was one of us. Johnston's face as she kicked at my fingers, attempting to send me to what could have been my death, was proof of that.

I sprinted into a nearby cluster of trees and crouched. I was left with only the sound of my heart beating in my ears and my own breathing. Utter and eerie quiet. Nothing came from the speaker in my helmet, and there was no readout in my visor.

Connection terminated.

I'd been cut off from the Sparrow. Nothing, including me, dared to move. The silence was terrifying, when I let my mind wander about how I was being watched by things I'd never seen before.

But gradually, Qav-4 answered the silence, breathing like a giant blinking away sleep and opening her eyes in the gleaming morning starlight. The planet came to life cautiously—brilliantly—in the tundra surrounding me, like a child's storybook had been opened before my eyes.

Rather than a single sun, a cluster of three large stars hung in the sky, which provided a worthy amount of light for the lush planet. Overhead, tiny, flying beasts flitted between branches in a canopy of green, purple, and blue boughs of faceted leaves. They chirruped to one another, clicking and popping in trills.

I placed a hand on a chalky, silver tree trunk, coming to my full height. Gossamer bloomed in silk webs, catching starlight in its nets. Bioluminescent beetles peered from darkened hiding places beneath fallen twigs and low brush, glowing amber and blue with small antennae bobbing in my direction. Curly-shelled snails clung to rocks and tree trunks, slicking their way to places I'd never know about. Unfamiliar scents hung on the air. The ground smelled rich, as if the soil held power and fertility. The atmosphere was fresh with humidity and moisture, a sense that mixed nicely through the heavy air. Water accumulated on thick leaves and dripped into mossy pools.

I stepped from cover, careful not to crush any of the beings with one of my thick-soled boots. Certainly other life forms watched me from hiding, so I proceeded back to the flattened circle where the Sparrow had set down, getting my bearings. My earlier path to discover the small brook was not far to the west. Remembering back to launch, TR.8B and I had run the same path briefly, same as the rest, before we splintered in different directions. 8B had gone off to the south at some point.

Hoping I would remember more, I started off at a run to the west. The path was fresh and familiar. Just minutes later, I arrived at the spring. I was stunned to realize I'd missed seeing a natural stone arch spanning the water just a few yards downstream. I lifted my visor.

Crafted of gleaming, pale, wind-napped rock, it was draped with creeping vines that thrust lavender blossoms upward against a blade of lichen that clung to the stone bridge. Beneath that, the brook tumbled gently into a pool where unseen things swam lazily beneath the surface, lost in the glare from ambient light, but for the ripples they caused with their leisurely movements. It was the most serene and beautiful place I'd ever seen.

Something white flashed to my left, then slammed into my ribs so hard it nearly took me off my feet. My side ignited with stabbing pain. Taken completely off guard, all I'd seen was a trail of motion from the trees. I recovered my composure, spinning to search through thick greenery for what had attacked me.

A SimNAC snarled and leapt, lightning fast, one of its grotesque, webbed claws digging into the armor atop my shoulder as it attempted to latch onto my head. I slammed a fist upward, smacking the sinewy alien in the chest and knocking it clear of me. It landed on its feet, stalking bipedally back and forth with a snarl on its pink-and-grey blotched face. It didn't attack, just sized me up as it paced, dark eyes analyzing me from my boots to the top of my helmet.

The beast's eyes locked on mine. It stared, cocking its head this way and that. A long, knotted mane of black hair slid across one shoulder. I was momentarily drawn back to an image of Johnston as she'd spoken and paced between us.

The SimNAC's watery eyes darted to the body of the one I'd exterminated earlier. It looked back at me, the grey lips surrounding yellow teeth, quivering with rage.

Or was it grief I saw?

I backed off a few paces. Keeping an eye on me, the SimNAC crept toward the body, hunching down next to it. Touching it. Cooing, then sobbing. Mourning its loss. I found it interesting how TRs had been conditioned to think of SimNACs as insects or pests when they were capable of emotion we're not supposed to have. I don't understand it, but my eyes grew wet when I saw it.

The longing to find my friend grew stronger. I dropped my visor and backed away while the SimNAC rocked and wailed, oblivious to me or the possibility that it could suffer the same fate as the other one.

I glanced away and scanned the brook again. I found that focusing on something, anything else, was preferable. The stream wove around stands of towering trees that were draped with thick, winding vines. The canopy was so dense in places that the starlight winked out overhead, leaving me in darkness.

I made my way slowly, listening to unseen creatures moving in every direction. They scattered when I tripped through a stand of spiky fronds. My guard was up as my visor blipped back and forth between day and night vision, depending on the deep, wet forest I navigated. Animals hooted and called in a trail of shrill alarms that echoed into the unseen surroundings. It was slow going, but I moved in the correct direction to intersect with B's earlier path.

I nearly tripped again, which was getting frustrating. My boot had grazed the unmoving foot of a fallen SimNAC. The creature was likely one of B's kills. I froze, glancing at the place where my boot rested next to the SimNAC's foot, which was bigger. A lot bigger. The muddy, clawed foot was attached to a muscular calf and thigh that led to a humanoid trunk, webbed arms, and head. The neck was twisted at an unnatural angle. There's no way it could function, let alone be breathing. Alive and standing upright on two legs, the thing would have been much taller than me. Disturbing as that knowledge was, it wasn't in my genetic makeup to feel afraid of a target, no matter the size or ferocity.

I adjusted my expectations, though. I did feel fear, but it wasn't for my safety. I was afraid for B. My mind kept recycling fearful thoughts of her lying injured somewhere that I couldn't see or get to. Worse, she could have suffered a fate similar to the dead terrestrial at my feet.

A trail had been beaten through the thick grass and vines, leading farther along the stream's course, so I followed it cautiously. The amount of traffic it took on a constant basis to render lush ground bare was substantial. The water flow had grown to that of a small river, covering the area with the soft whooshing sound of thestream coursing through a gravel bed and hissing through long blades of grass that clung to the bank. New species of crawling and slithering creatures made themselves evident as I walked and climbed over rocks, most of them more curious about me than afraid of a new element among them. Some slid on their moist bellies, some had appendages that they used to paddle their webbed feet along the ground, sometimes slipping into the water.

I kept a keen eye out for signs of my friend, but, at the same time, I was on guard against an attack. A sound like a deep, male voice talking behind a wall close by came from ahead, where there was a turn in the trail as it led out of sight. I stopped, listening hard and wondering if I'd really heard anything at all. I could have reasoned it away. Hearing a humanlike voice on an uncivilized planet could have been the creation of my emotional state. It came again, mixed with voices of differing timbres. In another world, those voices would indicate that there could be a crowd talking in a clearing. My mind churned with the thought that one of those who spoke could possibly be B, but who would the others belong to? Only one of the TRs from the jump hadn't made it to the Sparrow in time to get back to the New Hope. Two, if I counted me.

I had to keep myself calm and reasonable, the way my training had taught me. I left the trail, ducking through trees and bushes. I had to gain a vantage point to see what I was dealing with. I saw movement through the brush, so I dropped flat and belly-crawled forward. I put down my visor out of habit, ready to record my findings. Of course, my tech had stopped transmitting the moment the Sparrow was no longer in range, so I couldn't record anything. At least the binocular lens continued to target. There were too many scraggly twigs in my way, so I broke them off quietly, snapping them inside my palm to muffle the clicks and pops. Finally, I had a clear view ahead. I was stunned to stillness. I'd happened across a group of SimNACs, engaged in what appeared to be the act of simply living. Outside the yawning, soot-blackened mouth of a rocky cave, they came and went, communicated with their clawed hands and guttural noises, and shared trinkets from one hand to another. Downed trees and branches were stacked up on one side of the clearing, along with a stack of rocks of various sizes, and what appeared to be plant debris. There were males, like the ones I'd seen before. I counted four of them in this cluster. At least eight of the beings were apparently females, according to the obvious mammary growths on their chests.

The things I found most fascinating were the little ones. Their children. Some were as tall as the adults' waists, and other little ones barely toddled, fell, uprighted themselves, and carried on. They drug sticks through the dirt, and chased one another, threw things, and sometimes let out whooping shrieks. They snarled, smiled, and laughed. I found myself grinning, even stifling my laughter at their antics. They were lithe little spritely creatures, skin as pale as moonglow, and hair as black as night. The females held tiny ones close, the babies sleeping in the cradle of their arms.

They didn't wear clothes or shoes. They didn't carry weapons or wear armor. They simply existed.

I stayed there watching them for too long. Once I was able to tear myself away from the only real family unit I'd ever seen in person, I scooted backward and finally stood, gazing at the trail leading back to where a dead SimNAC lay face down, its head having been twisted to break the neck; an efficient kill by one of my sister units. Sadly, I guessed it was likely the work of TR.8B, as she'd followed the Parents' orders. I couldn't think about that, force myself to place blame. I, myself, had killed hundreds of SimNACs while fulfilling my duty on the other three Qav stars. Today alone I'd likely taken down at least 23, counting the one who'd been guarding the spring.

Or maybe it hadn't been guarding the spring at all. I broke into a sprint, closing the distance between the family camp and the large, dead SimNAC I'd found. When I got to the body, I turned in the direction of the spring I'd documented and ran quickly until I came to the body of the last terrestrial I'd dispatched. The kill replayed in my mind's eye. I noted the way I'd terminated it on the well-worn path that led to the camp. Looking back, I was sure that's what it was protecting. It had been guarding that family. Having someone to protect, something to die for, made them far more dangerous than before. The enemy threat was much more serious than what TRs had encountered on any of the other Qav planets.

The sound of rocks and dirt tumbling brought me back to the moment. The noises came from a stand of young trees ahead and to my right, creeping from beneath them in a mix of clacking stones and soft grunts. I braced against a tree trunk and peered over the edge of a jagged cut in the ground, surprised to see TR.8B far below at the bottom of a ravine where the soft edge fell down onto her as she attempted to claw her way out. B saw me then, and she lifted her visor, her eyes wide in the darkness of the hole she'd slipped into.

"TR.8C," she whispered loudly. "You didn't make it back to the Sparrow, either."

"I..." My voice simply dissipated on the air. Telling her I'd bailed off the Sparrow to find her wasn't what she needed to hear. I nodded. "And here we are. Together."

"The ground is unstable. Stay back, or you'll be stuck down here with me." She grinned. "I'm so happy to see you."

Relief washed over me. "I'll get you out," I said. "I'm glad I found you."

"Be careful. The SimNACs are huge."

"I saw the dead one. It's enormous," I said. "There are more. And I don't think this sinkhole is natural," she said, looking around her at the muddy walls. "I think this is a trap."

"What do you mean? That the SimNACs dug it out?"

She nodded. "There are horizontal claw marks from digging. The dead one tried to shove me down here before I killed it. I was off balance and slipped over the edge afterward."

If that was the case, the SimNACs were capable of much more than the Parents gave them credit for. I didn't want to think what they would do with whatever creature fell into the trap, but my mind whirled with possibilities. Everything needs to eat. Possibly, the trap was a means of harvesting prey. I shook it off and got back to the task of freeing my friend. "We can figure that out later. I'm going to get something to pull you up."

"Behind you!" B shouted.

At B's warning, I spun just in time to take a glancing blow off my helmet. Across from me, another mammoth SimNAC grunted as it regained its balance, readying the tree it had swung at me for another strike. There was no way something that topped three meters should have been able to sneak up on me. The tree glanced off the top of my helmet instead, throwing me off balance for a second. The SimNAC grunted, regained its balance from the swing, and held the club over a shoulder to strike again. I sidestepped away from the sinkhole to avoid falling, careful to keep my eyes on the snarling beast. It didn't advance, just glared over its stubby nose and locked, protruding jaw.

I had to crane my neck to look up into its face. The SimNAC had to be over three meters tall. Out of habit, or maybe it was duty, I touched a pad in my cheek with the tip of my tongue, attempted to click off a series of images with my visor, but the lens didn't respond. The idea that we'd been cut off by Johnston already, written off as dead or lost, chilled me. That was the only reason my tech could have stopped working, considering I was undamaged. Any drop to Qav-4 couldn't be thought of as a mission of extermination, considering how the indigenes had evolved. There was no way to send a warning to the Sparrow, an unfortunate effect of the Parents' policy to leave expendable TR units behind. The Parents don't believe in rescue missions.

That didn't really work for me anymore.

I swung my rifle into a solid grip and leveled it at the SimNAC, then squeezed the trigger. Nothing happened. Just a series of shallow clicks came from the weapon.

"Perfect," I growled. I dropped the rifle and used the strap to slide it around to my back, out of the way. That left my field knife as my only weapon. The SimNAC's club had to go, and I needed to get the beast in motion to do it. Many times in the past they'd been easily baited to get them out into the open during the cleansing of a site. This one seemed to be less prone to haste.

Careful to stay outside the SimNAC's reach, I circled the beast about four meters away, doing my best to seem ominous and threatening. I faked a step as if I intended to rush it. That got the response I needed. The SimNAC brought its club upright as it emitted a throaty, hissing noise and snarled, then stomped one of its enormous, filthy feet at me.

The lips curled upward, showing yellow-brown teeth.

That was a new dynamic. Never had a SimNAC toyed with me. It grinned menacingly. That display changed things. No longer was I dealing with a puny terrestrial being that would take no time to dispatch. We'd terminated enough of the SimNACs to build colonies on Qav-1, 2 and 3. Qav-4 might kill me, instead.

The SimNAC hoisted the tree well above my head. I lunged forward, drawing my field knife at the same time, and flipped the blade downward in my grip. By the time the SimNAC's club was in motion, slicing through the air directly at where my face would have been, I was well beneath the thing's strike range. It tried to stop the swing, but it was too late. I targeted its lead leg and sliced into the inside of the thigh as I ran low between its legs. The wound was a real gusher, but not the disabling strike I needed it to be. The mammoth howled when I cut through the sinew at the back of its knee. One of the massive hands came free, grabbing at me and digging its claws into the armor at the crook of my neck and collarbone. It snagged the strap to my rifle and jerked me backward.

I found myself dangling. I tried to keep my feet beneath me to remain upright, but the monster drug me from one side to the other, shaking me like I weighed nothing. It hoisted me off the ground, lifting me up like a duffle bag with my legs swinging. I shoved my free hand between my neck and the strap, then used my knife to hack through it while the SimNAC tossed me around. It was slow going, and I had to start over a few times. Finally the strap snapped, and I dropped face first to the turf. I rolled as far and as fast as I could, like a log headed downhill. I came to a crouch with the knife held ready to strike. The SimNAC grunted, looking at the rifle in its grip. It held the barrel end pointed at its chest. Sadly, the trigger wasn't working or even on its radar. It heaved the rifle into the thick overgrowth, then sprinted toward me.

I was on my feet and ready for a fight. The only tool the beast had was brute strength. It charged me, but I was small and fast in comparison. I dodged left as it ran past, then jammed my blade into its lower back. With an enraged yelp, it turned quicker than I expected and a blocky fist connected with my ribcage. My armor took some of the blow, but not enough to stop me from getting slammed sideways and having the wind knocked out of me. Somehow, I remained on my feet and managed to get a look over my shoulder just in time to see the SimNAC grab at me and lock its arms around my midsection. The pressure was intense, and I bit back panic, hacking at its shoulder and neck with the field knife. Deadly claws screeched across the plating protecting my chest and back.

I planted both feet and dropped low, as far as the monster's grip allowed, then drove both fists upward to break the thing's grip around me. My left batted one arm away, and my right smashed against the SimNAC's boney jaw. I attempted to spin away, but it snagged my legs and ripped my boots upward, sending me face first to the ground. My field knife flew from my grip and landed in a pile of leaves well out of reach. I spit dirt and shook my head to quiet the ringing in my ears. I got my knees under me, then kicked out to sweep the SimNAC's legs at the ankle. It hit the ground in a heap, and I lunged for my knife, but the beast caught my boot, and I hit the dirt again. I kicked free of its grip.

We both leapt to our feet, breathing hard and sizing each other up. It swung at me with one fist, which I dodged, but it latched onto my vest with its other hand. I jumped forward and up, cracking the thing's face with the flat of my right elbow. Stunned, the monster loosened its grip. I took two steps back defensively, transferred all the weight I dared, and side-stepped into a mean side kick, my boot crushing into the mass of dark hair between the hominoid's bleeding legs. It let out a sick grunt followed by a whooshing gasp, grasping at its abdomen and hunching. It was a dirty strike, but there were no rules in self-defense. Training for the fight in the name of conquest for the survival of my parent species worked that way.

While the creature was stunned, I kept momentum with another side kick into its ribcage. A rewarding snap popped against the outer blade of my foot. The SimNAC wheezed and curled into the blow. The thing's time was up. I had more important tasks ahead, like helping B. I sprinted to retrieve my field knife, circled quickly to the gasping beast's back, sank one hand into the greasy scalp full of matted hair, and drew my blade through the soft tissue of its throat. The dying animal grasped at its neck.

Blood erupted like a geyser through its fingers as I shoved it away. My breath came in ragged gasps as I stepped back. I bent, resting with my hands on my knees. Never had I fought with such a gargantuan. I'd never even seen such a huge alien. The thing died hard, clawing at the grass and growling as it bled out. It was the hardest fight I'd ever had. And I knew there was no way it was the only one of its kind.

I glanced over a shoulder at the dark places beneath trees and in the black shadows cast by rock outcroppings. There were likely hundreds of them out there watching. Finding safety was my new priority.

"TR.8C?" B's voice tumbled out of the ravine. I'd been so caught up in gaining new perspective that I'd forgotten my friend was stuck in a hole. I knelt and wiped my blade across the SimNAC's clumpy, matted hair to clean the blood off, then secured it in the sheath at my hip.

"I'm here," I said in a shaky voice. I walked to the big ditch, searching the pit for B. She was at the side closest to where I'd fought off the SimNAC, eyes wide with worry.

"We've got a problem out here," I said.

"Yeah." She nodded. "And you have a bloody nose and a split lip."

I laughed. "Yeah, I do. I'll be right back." I searched for the discarded tree the SimNAC had been using and found it nearby in a tangle of ferns. I dragged it over to the ditch and dropped one end to the uneven floor. B grabbed it and jammed the trunk against the far wall as I turned away to find the ne

arest group of vines. I found them hanging in clusters from a stand of trees by the riverbank. Ropey vines hung from the branches far above my head, where bright sunlight beamed down. The rays warmed the exposed skin of my nose and jaw. I tipped my head back and lifted my visor, letting the golden rays coat my face, allowing myself to breathe for a moment in the light. It was grounding, allowing myself to feel as I got my bearings. Tension formed a knot in my chest, which worked its way into my throat. I swallowed hard, tamping it back down with a locked jaw. I would be strong. Qav-4 offered survival, but it wouldn't be easy. We had a lot of work to do in order to stay alive.

I paced to the trees, unsheathed my field knife, and hacked down one of the thick vines. Freeing the base was easy enough. I had to climb one of the trees to get enough length to reach B. I worked fast, eager to help B out of the ravine. Back at the trap, I dropped the end down to her. She placed a foot on the trunk of the propped tree and nodded to signal she was ready. I sat down and dug my heels into the dirt and grass to brace myself as she pulled herself up.

B topped the soft edge with a relieved smile. We paced a few meters from the hole.

"Thanks. My hands were getting sore from digging. It wasn't doing any good." She dropped to the ground and scooted close, back-to-back with me so we could guard ourselves.

"I had a lot of time to think while I was stuck down there."

"Me, too. New Hope. All of them. They'll be back," I said. And it wouldn't be long. The Parents needed the water I'd found on Qav-4 to survive. They needed fresh air that wasn't compromised by the disease threatening to kill off the remaining few hundred of them on New Hope. The environmental system on the station was also on its last leg.

"It won't be a rescue mission on their part," she said. "It could be on ours."

"You're right. We are our own salvation. And we have their water." I nodded. "Our water."

"What happened to your weapon?" she asked.

"It jammed. Or the tech quit. I don't know. That SimNAC tossed it off in the brush over there. I'll find it."

"I ran out of ammo. Mine's stashed by the stone bridge." We sat in the healing quiet, resting and reflecting as starlight waxed and waned.

B spoke up after a few moments. "You know, we could show the others that there's another way. That it's okay to care about other TRs."

It was like she'd been mulling over our last conversation before we prepared for the drop earlier."That's taking a big risk."

"We've been taking risks since forever, and so has everyone else. They have to be just as tired of it as we are."

I nodded, smiling back at her. I'd grown thirsty. "Let's get a drink," I suggested.

"Yes," B agreed. After I dug my malfunctioning weapon from the brush, we found the trail and took turns drinking our fill beside the stone bridge and pool I'd found.

"I think the best thing we can do is secure and hold the landing site. They'll be back soon." I considered that for a moment. She was right. We could do that, but we'd have to hide when they offloaded the New Hope. And I didn't have a better idea.

"It will be very soon. The Parents are dying up there." I tossed away a twig I'd been toying with. "I found a family of SimNACs," I said, "with young ones."

"Interesting." B sat her helmet aside and cupped water onto her face and scalp. She glanced at me as if to speak, but then shook her head. "Hopefully they've moved on." I nodded. We took to the trail again, and before long, we made it back to the flattened turf and dead SimNACs that littered the site where the Sparrow had landed before.

"These are fairly small." B gestured toward the carnage.

"Well, let's clear the site." I grabbed the feet of the nearest dead SimNAC and dragged it to the base of a stand of trees. The start of decay did not improve its smell. B followed up with another, which we stacked on top of the first one. We kept dragging them off, which took a while. There was no hurry between us. We took turns getting water from the spring nearby. We rested. We waited. A while later, B sat forward.

"There," she said, pointing to the sky.

I dropped my visor to shield my eyes. Silhouetted against starlight, the Sparrow came into view as it dropped closer and prepared to land. We walked to a large tree that was close enough for us to observe the landing from a sheltered place. The engines screamed loudly, and landing gear protruded from the belly of the Sparrow. We leaned against the tree, waiting and watching as the bay door dropped.

A team of TRs in full gear sprinted down the ramp and onto the surface, their boots beating against the ground. Seeing them again was exciting and terrifying at the same time.

A single SimNAC appeared, drawn by the sound of the ship's engines. It was the first of many, although I wasn't worried about my sister TRs. Soon a few more followed, quickly taken down by gunfire. More appeared, and the TRs did what they were trained to do.

"I don't recognize a single one of them," I whispered.

B shook her head. "Do you think Johnston terminated our team because of us?"

"I wouldn't be shocked." The Sparrow's engines fired. Slowly, the bay door closed, sealing the TRs outside on the ground. As the dropship rose, a fresh onslaught of SimNACs surged from the trees. Some dropped from above and glided down onto the TRs, who were ready and waiting. We turned from the slaughter and sat with our backs against a boulder.

"I truly hoped to see 8S."

B simply nodded. She pulled her knees to her chest and rested her chin there. "We should go. We've got work to do.”

* * *

The Sparrow came and went with the days and weeks. B and I spied on the TRs as the camp grew in numbers, and the footprint of "civilization" spread like the splatter of a giant's blood in a mud puddle. Frail NonAugs arrived and kept to the shelters. I hoped the chance of a cure worked so well it created a sense of gratitude in them, one so strong it opened their hearts.

Sometimes hopes are like dreams. I wouldn't hold my breath and wait for a change in their attitude toward TRs. The SimNACs moved off farther and deeper into the trees. B and I kept track of their camps. Unknowingly, they taught us about food, and B and I took turns trying to make sure that the seeds, leaves, and wood pulp they harvested were safe for us to eat, too. I was thankful it was about survival and not a flavor palette.

Despite flavorless or bitter food, B and I did more than merely survive, however. We built a small hideaway in the safety of a cut in a rock wall. Our shelter was the first thing we'd ever created. We had walls, and all we needed to build was a roof. It was an easy first step for us and gave us a great source of purpose.

After that we used our blades to carve all manner of tools and supplies. B engineered an alarm system from thin vines and hollow pieces of wood. We mimicked items from back on New

Hope and created what we needed or wanted using wood, rocks, dried mud, and vines. We played games and talked ab

out books we'd read and programs we'd seen. We were happy together and unashamed of it. The other TRs living in the growing colony were not. Just like before on New Hope, they broke away in pairs or small groups and crossed the perimeter to get away from NonAug mandates. B and I enjoyed watching their happiness and exploration from a distance. Frequently, we saw them downstream from where the colony had claimed the stone bridge and pool.

The flow of the trickling brook grew to a wider river that roared and tumbled. The considerable noise created a safety issue. Whenever we neared the riverbank, one of us kept watch while the other drank and washed to ensure we weren't ambushed.

A pair of TRs beat us to our favorite slow pool along the river one afternoon. B saw them before I did and pulled me to a stop. We crouched in the shadow behind a massive tree trunk.

B sighed. "It would be interesting to talk with them, you know?" she whispered.

"Yeah. I wish we could trust them to keep us a secret." I was too far away to make out any distinguishing characteristics of the two. "I wonder if we know them."

"I can't tell," said B. Both TRs dropped their weapons and gear and shucked clothing. They looked around cautiously while they did it, but then appeared satisfied they were alone.

"They've grown complacent."

B nodded her agreement. She tapped my forearm and gestured high to my right. I followed her line of sight into the canopy of heavy branches of a nearby tree. A SimNAC slipped from its perch. It spanned its arms wide and glided silently to the ground, oblivious to the TRs. "Damn," I mumbled. The SimNAC stayed at a distance from them, but I knew too well how fast it could advance if it chose to. The way it crouched low and watched them worried me, too.

"That's a big one. Maybe it'll move off to another watering hole." It never hurt to hope.

"They'll see it," B whispered in clipped words. "Surely, they'll see it."

A second SimNAC broke from the trees. It scurried through grass and brush to crouch next to the other one. B saw it at the same time I did and grabbed my forearm.

"This is the first time I've seen the big ones pair up. We have to do something." Her voice came in a rush of panic. We were closer to the TRs than the SimNACs, which hadn't made a move. B and I both had our field knives, but we'd left the single functional weapon and few remaining rounds at our shelter. It would have been great if one of the TRs would stand up out of the water to get a good look around. For them, the bank was high enough to hide the threat.

But the SimNACs forced my hand. They slunk closer to the bathing TRs and gained speed with their advance. I unsheathed my blade. The sound of B sliding hers from the scabbard followed. We glanced at one another for a millisecond before coming to our feet and sprinting from the shadows and into the open.

"Hey!" I shouted to get the SimNACs' attention.

B had always been just a little faster than me. She targeted the closest of the pair as we closed distance to about 20 meters. I went for the second one. My feet seemed to work in slow motion. I couldn't get there fast enough.

The TRs heard me yell and splashed about as they stood up in alarm. One of the SimNACs turned toward B and me, but the other came to full height and broke into a sprint toward the surprised TRs.

One of our sister units lunged from the water and skittered forward to grab her weapon. She didn't bother coming to her feet, just propped it on the bank to take aim. She dropped the approaching SimNAC with a precise shot. That left one alien, the one B was after. The TRs were no longer in danger.

I turned to sprint after B, who grappled with the remaining SimNAC. The thing had wrapped her up in its sinewy, webbed grip. She struggled to move, but still managed to sink her blade into its abdomen, which didn't stop the beast from tearing at her. My view of B was partially obscured by the membrane between the SimNAC's arms.

I was nearly there. Panic and rage mix well in the right circumstances. I leapt at full speed, hit the SimNAC from the side, and wrapped my arms around its neck, as B ripped her blade from the thing's gut. She cried out when the SimNAC bit into her shoulder. We all toppled to the side, but the SimNAC shoved one massive leg out to stay upright. I was a spider monkey on its huge shoulders, with my legs trapping one arm, and an arm wrapped around its forehead. The SimNAC pitched backward and smashed me against the ground. It let go of B as it thrashed. The impact knocked the wind from my lungs, and I bit through the inside of my bottom lip, but I held my grip, wrapped around the greasy, stinking head. My chest burned like I might never pull in a full breath again, but the weight of the field knife in my right fist was reassuring. I spun the hilt carefully in my grip. With the blade pointed inward, I jammed the tip into the SimNAC's face just above and right of the nose, where its eye should be. I couldn't see a clear target and had to go by feel. It let out a screech, but I couldn't rest assured I'd killed it, so I yanked the blade free and stuck it again, again, and again. It thrashed until one of my legs came loose, and then it dropped, like an axe felled a tree. The beast's body weight dropped onto my hips, and the head rested against my chest. I dropped the back of my head against the grass and panted.

B untangled herself from the lax limbs. She growled and yanked one of the SimNAC's arms to pull it onto its side and free me.

"Stinking piece of trash," she grumbled. I pushed my way to sitting as B unleashed her rage on the dead SimNAC, kicking it over and over again. She finally stopped and caught her breath with her hands on her knees.

"Are you two okay?" A TR pulled her shirt over her head as she approached. The second one trailed her cautiously, her weapon at the ready.

B whirled on them. "You can't drop your gear and take a nice, leisurely swim here!" she shouted clipped words at them. "That was easily the stupidest thing you can do. If TR.8C hadn't yelled, you both could have died."

"TR.8C?" the leading TR asked. A glimpse of recognition flickered in her eyes. She turned to B. "TR.8B." A grin spread across her face. "B for short." Still rattled, B didn't return the smile.

The second TR stepped forward. "TR.8N," she said, gesturing to her friend, "and TR.8X."

"I thought I recognized you," I said. "It feels like it's been a year, if it's been a week."

"You must come back with us and see the colony," N said. Her excitement was genuine, although she didn't realize the depth of what it would mean for us to go back with them.

"That's suicide, and you know it." B crossed her arms over her chest.

N looked at the grass where pungent SimNAC blood had splattered and pooled. She nodded. "I hadn't thought of it that way."

"How did you do it? I mean, out here without the Parents and Mother?" X asked.

I smiled, glancing at B. "We survived."

B and I said goodbye and turned to the trees and shadows.

As we disappeared into our new realm of freedom, X's voice followed us. "If they can do it, we can, too."

The End

About the Author

Marie Whittaker enjoys teaching about publishing and project management for writers. She works as Associate Publisher at WordFire Press and Executive Director at Superstars Writing Seminars. She also puts in time as personal assistant to Kevin J. Anderson. In 2021, she co founded the epic fantasy world of Eldros Legacy. Marie is an award-winning essayist and author of horror, fantasy, children's books and supernatural thrillers. She is the creator of The Adventures of Lola Hopscotch, is published in Weird Tales, and habitually adopts rescue animals. Find out more about her at mariewhittaker.com .

www.ingramcontent.com/pod-product-compliance
Lightning Source LLC
Chambersburg PA
CBHW032256070726
47590CB00016B/2941